CYNDY SZEKERES'
Favorite Two-Minute Stories

Eight Stories Featuring Lovable Fuzzy Friends

W YORK
Wisconsin 53404
d in the U.S.A.
ssion from the publisher.
tern Publishing Company, Inc.
07-62187-1 (lib. bdg.)

Nothing-to-Do Puppy

Mama is away.
Daddy is dusting.
"There's nothing to do!" squeals Puppy.
Daddy thinks for a minute.
"You can start a Nothing-to-Do Club," he says.
"I will put up a tent for your clubhouse. You find
someone to join your club, someone who has nothing to do."

Puppy asks Pussycat to join his club.
"I can't," says Pussycat. "I am looking at my favorite picture book. Would you like to look, too?"
Pussycat shares her book with Puppy.

Puppy asks Mouse to join his club.

"Not now," says Mouse. "Mother is playing her fiddle, and I am going to dance. Will you dance, too?"

Mouse and Puppy dance.

Puppy asks Squirrel to join his club.

"I can't," says Squirrel. "My brother has a new ball and we are playing catch. Will you play, too?"

Squirrel and his brother play ball with Puppy.

At home, Daddy has the tent all ready.

"Did you find someone to join your club?" he asks.

"No," says Puppy with a yawn. "But I have something to do now."

"What is that?" asks Daddy.

Puppy wiggles into the tent.

"Nap," he says. "Having nothing to do has made me very tired!"

Sammy's Special Day

Today is a special day. Thumpity is coming to Sammy's house to play with him. When Thumpity arrives, Sammy tells him, "We will play in my room.

"Don't touch my truck," Sammy says.

"Leave my blocks alone," Sammy says.

"I will choose a game to play," Sammy says.

"I will have the first turn," Sammy says.

"Saved seat!" hollers Sammy. "You can sit on the floor."

Thumpity goes into the kitchen. One big tear slides down his cheek and off his whiskers.

"May I sit at the table until my mama comes for me?" Thumpity asks with a sigh.

"Of course," says Sammy's mama.

Thumpity kneels on the blue chair that belongs to Sammy's papa. He pulls some crayons out of his pocket. Sammy's mama gives him paper to draw on.

"How do you make flowers?" he asks Sammy's mama.

She draws two wonderful flowers for Thumpity. He draws ants and butterflies on them.

Sammy goes into the kitchen.

"I am not having any fun," he whimpers.

"Toys are not fun," says Mama. "Playing with them is fun. Sharing them with a friend is the most fun."

"Would you like to draw with my crayons?" Thumpity asks Sammy. Sammy draws a shining sun and a big rainbow.

"Would you like to play with my blocks?" Sammy asks Thumpity.

"Okay," says Thumpity.

"You can sit in my chair," Sammy says.

Sammy and Thumpity build bridges. They play games and take turns being first.

Soon it is time for Thumpity to leave.

"Good-bye," says Thumpity when his mother comes for him. "I will come back again, and you must come to play at my house."

Sammy and Thumpity give each other a big hug.

Scaredy Cat

Fuzzy and Scratchy and Scaredy were playing in the yard when something went, "Scritch, scritch, screech!"

"Meow! Meooow!" cried Scaredy Cat.

"Don't be frightened," said Fuzzy and Scratchy, laughing. "It is only a cricket. We're not afraid."

Suddenly the kittens heard another noise.

"Too-eet! Too-eet!" came from the air, and a feather dropped from the sky.

"Meow! Meooow!" cried Scaredy Cat.

"Don't be frightened," said Fuzzy and Scratchy, laughing.

"It is only a bird. We're not afraid."

Then "Ooooooh, oooooeeeh," whistled all around them.

"Meow! Meoow!" cried Scaredy Cat.

"Don't be frightened," said Fuzzy and Scratchy, laughing.

"It is only the sound of the wind. We're not afraid."

"*Balump! Bump! Bump!*" Something fell from a tree.

"Meow! Meooow!" cried Scaredy cat.

"Don't be frightened," said Fuzzy and Scratchy, laughing.

"It is only Mama's apple basket. We're not afraid."

Then something big and dark waved at the three kittens.
"Fullap! Fullap!"
"Oh! Oooh! Meow! Meoow!" cried Fuzzy and Scratchy.

"Don't be frightened," said Scaredy Cat, laughing. "That is only our quilt on the clothesline. Mama hung it out to air. I'm not afraid."

And she wasn't. So she changed her name to Velvet Paws!

Puppy Too Small

"I'm too small!" wailed Puppy. "I can't pull my toy box."

"But you can pull my wagon full of dear ones," Mrs. Bunny said. "Would you, please?"

And Puppy did.

"I'm too small!" wailed Puppy. "I can't climb the tree."

"But you can swing from it," said Squirrel. "Please swing with me."

And Puppy did.

"I'm too small!" wailed Puppy. "I can't dig a big hole to play in."

Chipmunk said, "This hole is just right for my acorns. Will you let me use it?"

And Puppy did.

"I'm too small!" wailed Puppy. "I can't carry my chair."

"But you can carry my sewing basket," said Grandma. "Please do."

And Puppy did.

Mama helped Puppy get ready for bed.

"Today," she said, "you have pulled a wagon full of dear ones, swung on a swing, dug a hole for acorns, and carried a sewing basket. Do you know why?"

"Why?" asked Puppy.

"Because you are just the right size!" And Mama gave him a hug and a squeeze.

And Puppy gave Mama a hug and a squeeze, too.

Melanie's Moving Day

Melanie Mouse is crying. Today is moving day. The Mouse family are leaving the farm. They will live in the woods. Melanie Mouse must say good-bye to all her friends.

"Oink! Oink! Oink!" all the piggies squeal. "Good-bye!" Melanie Mouse will miss her friends. So she sobs a big sob.

Mama and Papa pull a big cabbage leaf. It is filled with pots and pans, chairs and tables, blankets and books.

"Woof! Woof!" barks Daddy Dog. "Wave bye-bye," he tells his puppies. "We will visit Melanie Mouse someday."

Along the way to the woods, the Mouse family meet the Bunnies and Chipmunks. They invite the mice to join their picnic and share their pies.

"Will you be our friend?" the two little chipmunks ask with a giggle. They give Melanie Mouse a nutshell wagon.

At last the Mouse family reach their new home.

"Welcome! Welcome!" some mice squeal. "We are your neighbors. We will help you unpack."

Each mouse carries something inside. There is a big room with a fireplace, a special place for pots and pans, and a special place for books.

But, best of all, Melanie Mouse has her own cozy room.
She shows her toys to her new friends. Melanie Mouse isn't
crying anymore!

Puppy Lost

Mama said, "Hold my paw, Puppy dear." Puppy didn't, and now Mama is lost!

"Mama, Mama," Puppy whispers. "Mama," he says out loud.

"I want my mama!" he cries.

"Can I help you find your mama?" asks the grocer.

"Have a cookie," says a nice lady.

"You can share my raisins with me," offers a little girl.

"Mustn't go with strangers," thinks Puppy. "I mustn't take things from strangers, either."

"No, thank you," Puppy says out loud. "I will walk through the store until I see my mama."

Puppy walks through the store and sees many things. Puppy sees apples. Puppy sees soap. Puppy sees noodles. Puppy sees brooms.

Puppy sees his mama!

"You were lost!" he tells Mama. "You must hold my paw, so you won't get lost again."

"That is a very good thing to do," agrees Mama.

Suppertime for Frieda Fuzzypaws

"Suppertime," Mama calls. She puts some macaroni and two beans on Frieda's plate. But Frieda is watching Papa take something out of the oven.

Papa has baked cookies!

"I'm not hungry," says Frieda, pushing away her plate. "But I will have a cookie, please."

"Cookies are for after supper," Papa says.

"This is my after supper," says Frieda, "because I'm not having any supper."

Mama says, "You may leave the table until you are ready for supper. After you eat, you may have a cookie."

Soon nothing is left on Frieda's plate!

"I'm done!" Frieda exclaims.

Papa and Mama give her a glass of milk, two cookies, and a big kitty kiss.

Good Night, Sammy

It is bedtime. Sammy is in bed. But he is not tired.
Sammy's blanket is not tired. It goes kickety-kick. His
doll is not tired. It goes bouncety-bounce. His chair is not
tired. It goes rockety-rock.

"I can't sleep!" Sammy calls to his mama and papa. "My paw is too noisy. It goes twitchety-twitch. My pillow is too squashy. MY TAIL IS BEING TROUBLESOME!"

Mama kisses Sammy's paw. It stops being twitchy. Papa fluffs up Sammy's pillow. He tells Sammy's troublesome tail a story.

"I'm still not tired," says Sammy. "Everything is wide awake."

"That's because everything needs a song," says Mama.
"Good night, Sammy's paws," sings Mama.
"Good night, Sammy's tummy," croons Papa.
"Good night, whiskery whiskers," sings Sammy.
"Good night, blinky eyes."

Papa is fast asleep!
Mama has fallen asleep, too!
Good night, everybody.
Good night, everything.
Good night, Sammy.